This is Jack and his black dog Mack.

Jack has a knack for forgetting things.

Mack has a knack for bringing
them back.

When Jack hit the ball with a WHACK...

Mack brought it back.

When Jack left his books in a stack…

Mack brought them back.

When Jack left his backpack beside
the track…

Mack brought it back.

When Jack left his bike in the rack...

Mack brought it back.

But when Jack dropped his
snack sack…

Mack did NOT bring it back!

-ack Word Family Riddle

Listen to the riddle sentences. Add the right lette
or letters to the -ack sound to finish each one.

1 The opposite of front is ____ack.

2 The books on my desk are piled in a ____ack.

3 The plate was so old, it had a ____ack.

4 Watch out for the lion! He might ____ack.

5 My pen is not blue. It is ____ack.

6 When I come home from school, I eat a ____ack.

7 To go on vacation, first we need to ____ack.

8 The train on the track goes clickety- ____ack.

9 The race cars drive fast around the ____ack.

10 The ducks at the pond don't meow, they ____ack.

Now make up some new riddle sentences using -ack

-ack Cheer

Give a great holler, a cheer, a yell

For all of the words that we can spell

With an A, C, and K that make the sound –ack,

You'll find it in Mack and pack and snack.

Three little letters, that's all that we need

To make a whole family of words to read.

Make a list of other –ack words. Then use them in the cheer!